Tanta Teva and the Magic Booth

By Joel Lurie Grishaver

Illustrated by David Bleicher

Alef Design Group

Library of Congress Cataloging-in-Publication Data

Grishaver, Joel Lurie.

Tanta Teva and the magic booth / by Joel Lurie Grishaver ;
illustrated by David Bleicher.

p. cm.

Summary: When Marc meets a strange little old lady in the woods at
night, she uses her magic sukkah to take him back in time, where he
learns things about Biblical history tht he never heard in Hebrew
School.

ISBN# 1-881283-00-3 : $11.95

1. Bible. O.T.—History of Biblical events—Juvenile fiction.
[1. Bible. O.T.—History of Biblical events—Fiction. 2. Time travel—
Fiction. 3. Jews—Fiction]   I. Bleicher, David, ill.   II. Title.

PZ7.G8879Tan   1992

[Fic]—dc20   93-13193

CIP

AC

Mother:

for memories of Peter Put-put

Chapter 1

MY NAME IS MARC (WITH A "C") ZEIGER. Having a last name that begins with "Z" means that you are always the last one to be called. Being last means that you do a lot of waiting. And that means that you have two choices: either you can spend lots of time worrying that **they** are going to forget about you, or, you can relax and let **them** worry about finding you when **they** are ready. I like to take it easy. Maybe that's why I get busted all the time.

This book started out as an essay I wrote for school. I got an "A" on the essay and my teacher wrote this note saying "Marc has a vivid imagination." The only problem is that this is a true story. Nobody believes me. You probably won't believe me either, but this story is true. The nice people who bought this story from me to make this book don't believe that this really happened, either. They just think it's a good story and that it will make them a lot of money. I guess that's the way it goes.

Anyway, this is my story—**Tanta Teva and the Magic Booth** by Marc (with a "C") Zeiger.

This whole adventure got started because I wanted my parents to buy me a VR hookup (a Virtual Reality mask and glove). VR is when you play computer games "inside the game" instead of just watching them. It has these goggles that let you see the universe of the game in 3-D and a glove that responds to what you do with your hand. It's much cooler than the light pen which Evan just got. I just had to have one. My parents said no. I asked again, the answer was still no. I dropped hints. They still said no. No matter what I did , my parents still said no.

Then I came up with one of my bright ideas. My bright ideas always get me in trouble. I figured that if I ran away from home for just one night, they'd blow their tops and ground me for a week or two.

Then after I moped around the house for a week or two, and really showed them that I was sorry, they'd cheer me up with a surprise VR kit. It was not one of my better plans, but I was too old to try crying. I waited and picked the right night. It was the night before the big spelling test (you know, the one that makes you remember all the words from the last nine weekly spelling tests). I packed a few things and got ready for my night in the woods.

I knew that I had to travel light. I didn't waste time getting the old Boy Scout compass or any of that stuff off the shelf. I only packed the essentials: my Walkman and four cassette tapes, a dozen comics, some peanut butter cups, chocolate bars, granola sticks (Okay, I know they're too healthy to really like, but I still like them), a six-pack of soda, my flashlight and three extra sets of batteries, my sleeping bag, a blow-up pillow and a foam pad. It all fit into my backpack. In the kitchen I added three sandwiches, a box of little donuts, and a can of Pringles. I didn't have room for my spelling book and I had to carry my sleeping bag in my arms.

I spent two days reworking this letter on the computer. *Bank Street Writer* makes it real easy. (If any English teachers are reading this book, I know that you are supposed to say "really" cause that's the adverb, but kids make fun of you if you talk like that.) I ran a copy off on the printer and stuck it under the pineapple magnet on the refrigerator.

Dear Mom and the Monster,

I know that you don't really love me. Well you won't have to be bothered anymore. I'm going somewhere where people will really love me. People who love people give them things that they really want. Good-bye forever.

Your X-son,

Marc.

I knew that the "X-son" part would really get to them.

Chapter 2

WE LIVE AT THE END OF THE STREET. Behind our house there are woods. I've spent my whole life playing **STAR WARS, TERMINATOR,** and fighting dragons in those woods. I know every place to hide, every single place to make an ambush, every single trail. I even know places that Evan and Sean haven't found. Besides, even though we call it "the forest," it's not. It's just a couple of blocks of trees which fill up the empty block between two streets. Somehow, this night when I was running away, I went into the woods and got lost. I mean, I found myself in a part of the forest where I had never been before. That's impossible because there are no parts of the forest where I haven't been, but that's what happened. My mother thinks it was just because it was dark and I got confused. Frankenstein still thinks that I bumped my head and dreamed the whole story. I still haven't figured it out.

Anyway, it was after dinner, it was dark and I was lost in a part of the woods which didn't exist. I figured: "No problem." I did the only logical thing. I talked to myself a little and kept walking along this trail. The trail ended in this clearing I'd never seen before. In the middle of the clearing was this funny green booth, and off to the side was a little old lady. Believe it or not, there was a cleaning-woman standing there trying to scrub the graffiti off of the rocks. The cleaning lady was muttering to herself: "*Shmutz, shmutz*, everywhere, *shmutz*. How am I supposed to keep the whole world clean if no one helps. I'll never keep this place clean."

She was a real sight, standing there in the lantern light, trying to scrub the spray-paint off those boulders. She looked like that character at the beginning of Carol Burnette (which you can now see only in reruns on cable channels over 30) except

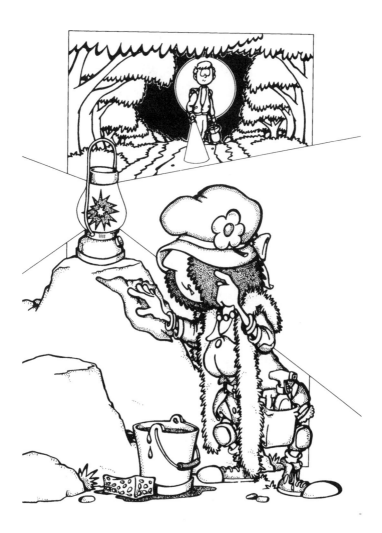

that she was very short. She was wearing
red sneakers, two different colored socks,
knee-pads, and an old patched dress. On
her head was this cloth cap which looked
like a calico shower cap with lace. She
really did look funny. I wasn't scared or
anything, but I did know that I was into
something weird. I left my things at the
edge of the clearing and sneaked closer.

When I got within eight or ten feet, this
cleaning lady did the funniest thing.
Without turning around or moving, she
suddenly said, "You can come closer. I
don't bite, and I'm not one of those little
old ladies who spits in her handkerchief
and then smears the dirt on your face."

I came closer. She said, "I'm Tanta
Teva, who are you?"

I introduced myself, "Marc with a 'C' Zeiger, ma'am." I know that it's funny to hear me call someone 'ma'am,' but what else do you call a cleaning lady who introduces herself as a "Tanta" in the middle of a clearing in the woods which couldn't possibly exist. I watched her work for a while, and then asked her why she had a booth made out of branches and covered in fruits and vegetables. She answered: "It's my sukkah."

I said, "Sukkahs are something you learn about in Hebrew school."

She said, "The plural is 'sukkot."

"Then why do you have a sukkot?"

"Sukkah," she corrected, and sprayed some more cleaner on the rock.

Then I repeated, "So why do you have one?" (I was smart enough to use 'one' and not give her another chance to correct me.)

She answered me with just two words: "Get in."

When I first told this part of the story at home, my mother started to smile and the monster told me that I had been to too many Steven Spielberg movies. I don't care what they think, this is what really happened. I walked over to her sukkah and saw that it was just this little booth, maybe three feet square and six or seven feet tall. It was sort of the size of a phone booth, except that it was made out of branches and all kinds of fruit and vegetables were hanging from it. It even had strings of popcorn and cranberries. I got into the booth and she followed me. Then the special effects started. At least in the movies it is always done with special effects; here, I don't know what happened. All of a sudden there was fog everywhere. Then bright white light started shining from everywhere around the sukkah. In the background there was this deep, deep rumble. Tanta Teva just stood there and smiled just the littlest bit, not saying anything. Then it was all gone.

Chapter 3

ALL OF A SUDDEN IT WAS DAYLIGHT. Bright daylight. It was the middle of the afternoon and it was hot out. I looked outside the sukkah and there were palm trees. It was desert outside. I couldn't help myself. I whispered, "Toto, I don't think we're in Kansas anymore." Next to that line in my

school essay, my teacher wrote "TOO
CUTE" in big red letters. But I really did
say it.

Tanta Teva looked at me and said two
more words: "Get out."

When I stepped outside the sukkah, I found that our booth was parked in a row of sukkot. In fact, there was even a sign overhead which said: **Zevulun's Wilderness of Sin Sukkah Park.** Joshua

later told me that the sign was just Zevulun's idea of a joke. As I walked away from Tanta's sukkah, I figured out that we were now in the middle of a big oasis somewhere in the desert. This was my first oasis. All of a sudden I heard shouting. Three big kids chased this little kid down the row of these sukkah booths. All four boys were wearing white skirts, gold and blue necklaces and eye makeup, but they weren't wimps. This was exactly what you'd expect Egyptian kids to wear in something hundred B.C.E. (I learned to say B.C.E. the hard way because one of my Hebrew School teachers made this big fuss that B.C. is Christian any time someone used it). Well, these weren't really Egyptian kids, they were actually escaped slaves, but I'm getting ahead of the story.

When Joshua came running down the street being chased by those three big kids (even though I didn't know that he was Joshua at the time), I thought they were chasing him for real. The three of them started sword-fighting against him with these swords made out of bamboo, so I grabbed this curved staff which they later told me was a shepherd's stick or something, and joined the fight. I thought that I got into the fight to help the little kid out. It turned out that he saved me, except that it was all for play and for training. Those big guys knocked me down three or four times, and Joshua beat them off me. Eventually they all just stood around me and laughed. What do you want—I haven't even been taking karate for a year yet. Frankenstein kids me that I've got my "pink belt." Actually it's still white.

The little kid who could really handle a sword introduced himself as Joshua, son of Nun. He thought Marc (with a "C") was a funny name. When I pieced the whole story together, I learned that Joshua and the other 600,000 people in **Zevulun's Sukkah Park** had just escaped a few weeks before from Pharaoh in Egypt. They had all been slaves and Moses had led them out. Joshua was really proud that he had been chosen by Moses to attend him. I never did figure out what kind of job "attending" was. It seemed funny to me that "X-slaves" were wearing lots of gold jewelry. When I asked Joshua, he explained that just before they left Egypt, Moses had told them to borrow gold and jewels from the Egyptians.

He said, "Now everyone has nice stuff to wear and we don't feel like slaves anymore."

When I let Evan and Sean read this story, they said that I just made it up out of stuff that I had learned at Hebrew School. Believe me, I didn't learn any of this there. If you don't trust me, ask any of my Hebrew School teachers. They'll swear that I couldn't have learned this much. I cause a lot more trouble there than I do in regular school.

While we walked around camp, Joshua told me lots of stuff. He explained that they spent almost every day fighting with bamboo swords, not so much because it was fun, but because Moses had ordered it.

Joshua said, "Free people have to be ready to defend their freedom."

"Why do you live in these sukkahs?" I asked Joshua.

"Sukkot," Joshua corrected me. "We live in them here in the wilderness because we don't have anything else. We left Egypt on a day's notice. I took my clothes, the gold necklace I borrowed on Moses' orders, and a bag with a few things that my father and my grandfather had carved for me. Then, my mother made me throw a warm cloak over my shoulder. In it she put bread dough she had just made. We didn't even have time to let it rise."

"Matza," I said.

"I thought that you didn't know anything about us?" Joshua asked.

I told him, "Never mind, its too hard to explain," and suddenly realized that I knew more than I thought I did about Jewish stuff.

Joshua showed me his real sword. It was made out of bronze.

"Why don't you use steel swords?" I asked. Joshua had never heard of steel. When I asked him about iron, he said, "Only the Sea People have iron swords."

"Who are the Sea People?" I asked

"A people who come from the sea. They sell themselves as soldiers and sailors."

"That much I could figure out myself. Who are they?"

Patiently Joshua explained, "The Sea People are this nation of warriors who come from this country across the Great Sea. For a couple of hundred years they've been landing their boats up and down the shore and conquering everyone. They are the only ones in the world who know how to make iron. Everyone else has to fight with either bronze or copper. When you hit a bronze sword with an iron one, the iron sword cuts into the other one. This is how they win so much."

When we went back to Joshua's sukkah, he showed me his little leather bag. He told me, "In here is the only thing I took out of Egypt for myself. In here are the reasons I believe in miracles. Open your hands."

I held my hands out like I was doing an Allstate Insurance ad and he began to dump out a bunch of little carved animals. I looked down and saw that there were two of every kind of animal. Some of them were carved out of wood; others were made from bones or ivory or something.

"Just like Noah's ark," I said.

"The ark is in here too," he said, "but how did you know the story?"

"We still tell it," I said. "My mother was the first one to tell it to me."

Joshua paused for a moment. His eyes filled with tears, and he said: "I never knew my real parents, all I know is that my grandfather made some of these for my father. My father made others, and all of them were left for me."

When Joshua walked me back to Tanta Teva's sukkah, I had a funny feeling thinking of the batteries and the Pringles, and everything I packed for one night in the woods when I compared it to Joshua's bag of animals and the matza dough he carried in his cloak.

When I got back to our booth, Tanta was waiting. I asked her, "Now do I know Sukkot?"

She looked at me and said those two words: "Get in."

I asked, "Do you always speak only two words?"

She answered, "Not always." She tried to keep this really straight serious face, but we both laughed. She said, "Let's go."

Chapter 4

 I GOT BACK IN THE PHONE- BOOTH-SIZED SUKKAH AND THE SPECIAL EFFECTS STARTED ALL OVER AGAIN. Near my home is this place called **Six Flags Magic Mountain** which is a park where they have lots of rides. One of the rides is this thing where they strap you on your back and then they push you off a cliff. The car slides down

on the track and you fall for maybe a quarter of a mile, and then the track curves and you eventually stop. They call this ride the **Freefall**. I hate those kinds of rides and I've only been on it once. That was when Evan and Sean called me a chicken. Anyway, once I got into the sukkah, and the fog came up, it felt like someone pushed us over the **Freefall** track. When everything stopped moving and glowing and the low rumbling sound stopped, I was lying on the floor looking up at Tanta who was sitting quietly at a small table. I looked outside and **Zevulun's Wilderness of Sin Sukkah Park** was gone. So was the desert.

Tanta smiled a little smirk and said, "This isn't Kansas either."

I got up, brushed myself off, and looked outside. We were on the edge of a barley field, at least I later learned that it was a barley field. Our sukkah was sitting at the end of a row which had four small sukkot, and a lean-to kind of thing. I took one step outside, and then WOOOSSSSHH. This rock flies past my face. Then, SMASSSSSHH, this pot sitting on a stone wall goes crash. When Frankenstein was helping me type up the book for the publisher, he said that I should have had David save my life with this shot and kill a snake. He said, "Make him a real hero, like Davy Crockett." I told him that wasn't the way it happened. He said, "Use literary license." I told him, "I'm too young to get a literary license." Besides, David was doing target practice with his sling, knocking broken pots off a stone wall the way gunfighters used to do with tin cans. I figured that was hero enough for me. Anyway, this rock whizzed past my nose and I was standing there with my mouth open, and this shepherd kid comes running up and starts to apologize.

David really did look like the kind of shepherd kid you always see in Christmas pageants, except that the clothes looked like he really wore them, and they weren't costumes or anything. He was wearing a brown skirt-like thing (my cousin Sally would call it a mini-skirt) with this sheepskin vest, and this great leather belt. On his feet he had the kind of sandals you always see in biblical movies. He didn't wear the headband kind of thing they always show you in the books. The funny thing was the ground-in dirt. I mean his face was clean and everything, but you could tell that he slept and worked outdoors.

On television shows like **Voyagers**, they make it real easy to travel in time. (**Voyagers** is another old show you can only see now on cable at six on Sunday mornings—or other times like that.) The kid on that show always knew the right thing to say. With David, I got almost nothing right.

He comes running up and says, "I'm sorry. I'm sorry. I didn't want to hurt you or anything. I just didn't see you until the rock was flying." He handed me this leather strap thing and said, "Go ahead, you fling one at me."

I said, "I don't want to hurt you either." Actually I had no idea what he wanted.

"Use it on me. We won't be even till you do."

I realized that he wouldn't give up, so I looked at the thing in my hand. It was a square of leather with two straps, one tied to each side. It looked like it was an eye-patch for the HULK, but that couldn't be, so I figured that it must be a whip. I made like Indiana Jones and lashed David across the back.

"Ouch," he shouted. "That hurt!"

"But you told me to..." I screamed and took two steps back.

"I told you to fling a rock at me! I'm fast enough to dodge anyone with a sling," he said, calming down a little.

"What kind of sling is this?" I asked. I still thought it was really an eye-patch.

"It's a great sling. My brother Shammah made it for me."

"Well it's not the way we make slingshots," I said. "We make ours out of a forked stick and a piece of tire." I had no trouble explaining the forked stick idea. Where I got in trouble was trying to explain how you take a rubber inner tube and cut out the rubber band part. In science fiction stories, they are always worried about changing history, but believe me, there was little danger of David opening the first branch of B.F. Goodrich in ancient Israel! We shook hands and then David showed me how to work the sling.

In science class we learned that the slingshot works because of Sir Isaac Newton: for every action there is an equal and opposite reaction. David's sling worked on centrifugal force. I guess it was the best they could do without rubber. You put a rock in the center and held the ends of the two straps. Then you spun the thing over your head, and when you were ready to shoot you just let go of one side. Letting go at the right time is the hard part. My first shot went backwards. The next one went straight up in the air and then back down and almost clobbered us. In forty or fifty tries, I didn't smash one of the cracked jugs on that stone wall.

At that point we got interrupted. David's grandfather called him from the field.

"I've got to go to work," he said, "you want to come help?"

Not knowing better I said, "Sure."

While we were walking I asked, "Which of these sukkot does your family live in?"

"You are weird," he said. "Do people live in sukkot where you come from?"

"No"

And he said, "Well, we don't either. We camp out in them when we're out working a harvest. That way we can put in a full day from sunup to sundown."

"Where do you live?" I said, trying to make conversation.

He pointed towards one of the hills and said, "Bethlehem." Then he asked, "And you?"

I said: "That's harder to explain than inner tubes."

At home, I always thought that work was stuff like mowing the lawn, taking the stack of papers in for recycling or washing the station wagon. I had no idea what it would be like harvesting a barley field. David's grandpa Obed handed me this curved knife for harvesting barley—I guess

we call it a sickle—and then put me in the field. David took one row and started hacking away at the base of a clump of barley. He cut down a small bunch and then tied it into a bundle. Then I started to work. I grabbed the top of the barley and cut it off halfway down the stalk.

Grandpa Obed yelled, "No, No, No! You're cutting it like an Egyptian. You're wasting half the stalk. In Egypt they are rich, they can afford to use only the grain. Here, we use it all. We eat the grain, the stalk feeds our oxen, and we even use the waste to make bricks hard. Let me show you."

I mumbled something about "bricks without straw." It was a phrase I knew by heart, but I didn't know from where. After a while, I got the hang of cutting the stalks, holding the pile in one hand, and then tying it in a bundle when I had enough. I was working and sweating, but not going half as fast as David. After a while this old woman began following me. Every time I dropped something, she would scoop it up and put it in her bag. It got me really angry. When we stopped for a break, I told David, "I know I'm just beginning to learn how to do this, but you don't need to put that old woman behind me. I'll go back and clean up."

David looked at me and laughed. "You really don't know anything. That woman is gleaning."

"Gleaning?" I asked.

"It's a law in the Torah."

I told him, "Torah I know, gleaning I don't know."

Then David quoted, "**When you reap the harvest of your fields, you shall not go back and gather up that which has fallen; leave it for the stranger, the fatherless and the widow**."

"How'd you know that by heart?" I asked.

"When I study with my father, I learn everything by heart. How does your father teach you Torah?"

I was a little embarrassed. "I don't live with my father. The Monster and I don't study together, and my Hebrew School teacher has us read out loud."

David shook his head and said, "The City is a strange place."

We went back to work. When we were almost at the end of our row, we came to this string which was tied diagonally across the corner of the field. I started to cut it. I pulled my hand back to hack it with my knife. David stopped me. "I was afraid you would do that. The string marks **Pe'ah**."

I said, "What?"

He said, "You know, the corners."

I said, "No I don't know. What corners?"

He said, "**And when you reap the harvest of your fields, you shall not totally harvest the field. You shall leave the corners of the field for the poor and the stranger**."

I said, "More Torah, right?"

David just smiled and went back to work. We moved over to the next row and started back down the field. My little old lady and two young girls were now happily following behind me. They had figured out that I was a good bet because I dropped a lot.

This was all I needed. My hands had blisters, my back hurt from bending over, I

had never been this sweaty in my life, and in spite of all this pain, what was I getting— Torah study! I had just about had it.

I dropped my last half-finished bundle and turned to David. "I've got to take a break."

He said, "Don't..." then said, "Never mind."

I said, "Don't what?"

He said, "Don't leave that bundle of grain in the field!"

I started to ask why, but then I turned to find my little old friend and the two young girls dividing my hard cut bundle.

I said, "What?"

David said, "**When you reap the harvest of your field and you forget a sheaf in the field, do not go back and get it, leave it for the**

stranger, the fatherless, and the widow."

I said, "More Torah, wonderful!" I was very sarcastic.

He said, "Don't worry about it. We always take good care of the gleaners because my great- grandpa Boaz met great-grandma Ruth when she was gleaning here in his fields." Then he said, "Let's quit for the day."

I said, "That's the best Torah you've said yet."

He just smiled. We went back to the sukkot. David showed me the place where he slept. He started to take out and tune his harp. He called it a harp, but it was more like a curved thing with a dozen strings than that triangular thing that angels play in movies. While he was tuning, I asked, "Tell me, how did you kill Goliath?"

He said, "Who? I've never killed anyone."

I said, "Goliath, the Philistine giant."

"The Philistines are slime," David said, "but I've never heard of a giant."

"Never mind," I said, "I must be confused."

David picked up his harp and started to play me this song he was writing.

"I'm a shepherd, I take care of my sheep.

God is a shepherd, he protects my sleep."

Then he said, "I'm still working on it."

I told him I knew two Jewish songs he should know. I sang **Hava Nagilah**, but he had never heard it before and I couldn't really say the words. I thought every Jew knew that song, but David evidently never went to Bar Mitzvah parties. Then I sang him **David Melech Yisrael** complete with the hand motions.

He laughed and said, "That's silly, Israel doesn't have a king. But you know what's funny? My mother used to sing me to sleep with the same words."

I realized it was getting late. I looked at the blisters on my hands and thought about the day. I really did hurt all over. I had a funny thought. I wondered how everyone would react if I walked into our grocery store and roped off each corner and put up a sign which read **Free to strangers, the poor and the fatherless**.

Then I figured that this bright idea would get me into a lot of trouble.

At the door, David said, "Tomorrow I'll show you my flock and we'll practice more sling."

I said, "Great! Then can we hang out at the mall?"

David asked, "Where is Mall?"

I said, "Don't worry about it, the Mallites are slime anyway." When Frankenstein read that joke, he added: "You should have added — 'all Mall is divided in three parts'." He laughed, but I didn't understand his joke. Maybe you can ask your parents.

I said goodbye to David, and told him, "Annihilate Goliath for me, when you meet him."

Then Tanta said her favorite two words, "Get in."

Chapter 5

Inside I asked her, "Now do I know everything about a sukkah?"

I can tell you her answer in two words: "Not yet."

I asked her, "Why do you always speak in two words?"

I didn't word the question right, but she understood.

Tanta answered, "No reason."

I got ready for our next trip. I braced myself in the corner and held on real good. On television shows they use the same special effects all the time. On MTV they always launch the same rocket ship, and on **Star Trek** they always show the Enterprise flying the same way. I figured it worked the same way in real life. But Tanta doesn't work that way.

She said, "Ready, Marc?" Just two words and no countdown. I shut my eyes. Then she said, "We're there." There was no flash, no tumble, no fog, no deep, deep rumble. We were just there. I looked outside and saw a sign: "**Honi's Holy City Sukkah Park**. Tanta looked at me and said, "Get going."

I walked outside into this sukkah park which was located just outside the walls of a big ancient city. I saw one kid standing by a tree. If I didn't know that I was supposed to be having a Jewish adventure, I would have figured from his clothes that I was in ancient Greece or Rome or someplace like that. I walked up to him and said, "I think we're supposed to meet. I'm Mar..."

He interrupted me, "Don't say anything yet. Stand on one foot, tell me who you are and what you're doing here."

I said, "I'm Marc with a 'C' and I'm here visiting." I didn't think that it would be a good idea to tell him that I had run away from home the night before a ten-chapter spelling test in order to manipulate my parents into getting me a

VR kit, but this cleaning lady with a magic sukkah has been bouncing me around history. It wouldn't have made sense in my day. In whatever year this was, who knows what kind of trouble I could be in? I

needed to change the subject. I said
quickly, "You do it."

He stood on one foot and said, "I'm
Hillel. I'm 11 years old. I'm studying to be
a Rabbi. I live near Jerusalem, and I am
here to meet the pilgrims."

None of this made sense. No one who is 11 wants to be a rabbi or could possibly study for it, and the pilgrims came to Plymouth Rock which was nowhere near Jerusalem. I was in trouble for sure. I asked him, "Why did we do this on one foot?"

Hillel laughed. "Oh, it's just a game I play with my friend Shammai. When we have an argument or just two different opinions, we could go on forever. So we started this game, that when you state an opinion you have to stand on one foot. That keeps it short."

"Or it means that you get to have a lot of opinions," I said. Hillel laughed.

I got an idea. "Let's see how good you are. I'll ask the questions for a while."

"No sweat," Hillel said.

"Where are we?"

"Just outside of Jerusalem."

"Why are pilgrims coming?"

"Tonight is Sukkot. It's the biggest Jewish holiday of the year."

I said, "You're wrong, Yom Kippur is the most important holiday." I knew that, because that was the only day of the year when I was sure my mother would let me stay out of regular school. I didn't know anyone who skipped school for Sukkot.

"Wrong," Hillel said, "Yom Kippur is only big stuff for the priests in The Temple. I mean, it's important and everything, but for the people, Sukkot is a big deal because it is Sukkot which brings the rainy season that makes crops grow well."

I decided to ignore the problem of what
was a Jewish priest. I knew we didn't have
any at my temple. But I did understand
the rainy season business. In these
latitudes it only rains during the winter
season. I remembered the chalk circles Mr.
Kelly drew on the globe to explain it.

Then Hillel said, "Come on, tourist, let me show you around some."

It was an incredible day. I can't remember it as well as the time with Joshua or with David. Too much was going on. It was like being a kid at a circus parade (only I've never been to a circus parade). People were coming into the city from all over.

Thousands of tourists were arriving. They called the tourists 'pilgrims,' but they were basically tourists. If someone had invented postcards he could have made a fortune. People were selling and buying things all over. In those days, the motel hadn't been invented either, so people camped out in sukkot all over town. **<u>Honi</u>'s Holy City Sukkah Park**, the cluster where we had landed, was only one of dozens (maybe hundreds) set up all over. It was a good deal. **<u>Honi</u>** made money and people had a place to stay.

I asked Hillel lots of questions, but I'm not sure that I really understood it too well. In those days there was only one Jewish Temple in Jerusalem and none in the towns or suburbs. There were some other temples but they worshiped idols or strange gods and were evil. That meant that Jews only came to services three times a year. I wish Rabbi Cutler knew that. She is still convinced that we should go every week. Except that services were really different then. Almost everyone was a farmer and you were supposed to bring this thing called tithes. Anyway, that's what set up the celebration. Jews came from everywhere and they brought gifts to the Temple so it would rain well and so that they would have more to bring next year. That almost makes sense.

What was great was watching people come into the city. It was almost like watching the Rose Parade on New Year's morning. I mean, there weren't floats or anything, but people came in singing and dancing. Everyone was dressed up. People were kissing and hugging everyone. It was the biggest party I'd ever been to. If everyone came to my synagogue in this kind of mood, I'd be happy to go all the time.

Hillel showed me all over. He wanted to take me to the Temple to show me where the water-pouring was going to take place. I didn't know what the water-pouring was, but it was the big thing. You had to stand in line for a day or two. Sounds as hard as getting **Guns & Roses** tickets. He was also going to show me where they juggled torches at night, so I could come back and watch them. That was supposed to be the best part of the whole thing.

Near the end of the day, Hillel turned to me and said,

"Stand on one foot and tell me what it is to be a Jew."

My only answer was, "What?"

He repeated, "Stand on one foot and tell me what it is to be a Jew."

I stood on one foot for a long time. After maybe a minute or two, I started to give one or two answers, then stopped myself.

Finally I said, "I don't know."

Hillel said, "I haven't got the answer either, but I've been thinking about it a lot."

Hillel walked me back to Tanta's sukkah, and then told me where to meet him if Tanta let me stay to watch the torch jugglers. We hugged good-bye.

ו

Chapter 6

 TANTA GREETED ME
WITH TWO WORDS,
"NICE DAY?"

I gave her a taste of
her own medicine. "Sure thing."

Then she said, "Hold on." This special
effect treated me to another ride on
Freefall. She threw in the lights, the fog,
the deep, deep rumble and everything.
This time we wound up in the middle of

nowhere—and I do mean literally in the middle of nowhere. I looked out and nothing was there. I don't mean it was just dark—it was total black nothing everywhere outside the sukkah.

Tanta said: "Marc with a 'C', please stand up, we're going to have company." I didn't move.

"Where are we?" I asked.

Tanta didn't answer, she just pointed up to the roof. I could see the stars. "You've got to have stars," she said.

I stood up, and a man in a long black robe entered. He had a hood over his head.

Tanta said, "Abraham, I want you to meet my friend Marc with a 'C'."

Abraham said, "Nice to meet you," and then proceeded to introduce his wife

Sarah, Sarah's handmaiden Hagar, and his servant Eliezer. I don't know what a handmaiden is, but I did know that this three foot by three foot by six foot sukkah was very crowded.

I asked Tanta, "What's going on?"

She answered, "Part of a sukkah is inviting special people. *Ushpizin* my boy, *Ushpizin*."

Another man appeared at the door. Tanta said: "Isaac, please meet master Marc with a "C'."

Isaac said, "The honor is mine." Then he introduced his wife Rebekkah.

At this point the sukkah was getting really crowded. I said Tanta, "I have got two words for you. You're crazy!"

It didn't stop her. In short order, she introduced me to Jacob and his thirteen children including Joseph with his many-colored coat. Moses came in (but he didn't bring the Tablets), and he introduced his brother Aaron. The last person I remember entering was King David. I really don't know where we put people. It seemed like there were people everywhere. I was wedged between Joseph and Eliezer, I never made it near David to find out if he was the same person I met earlier.

When my mother heard this adventure she laughed and said that when she was in college they used to have contests like this. People used to see how many people they could squeeze into a phone booth. She explained that it was a fad, like eating goldfish. I told her that I'd stick to just piercing my ear. She yelled something. Wearing an earring is just something to threaten her with. Evan has one, but I'll never do it.

When Frankenstein typed this part, he said it was just like a scene in some old Marx Brothers movie. The Marx Brothers are in a bunch of old black-and-white comedies that he likes. I think they're boring. Everything in black-and-white is boring. When I asked him how they got everyone out of the room, he said that someone opened the door and everyone fell out. I don't know how I got out of the sukkah.

Chapter 7

THE NEXT THING I REMEMBER IS WAKING UP THAT MORNING IN THE CLEARING. This time I even recognized it. I know you'll all say that this was a dream, but explain this: what happened to all the graffiti on the rocks?

When I got home, I found this note under the pineapple magnet:

Dear "X-Son",

Hope you had a nice night. We had to leave for work – but you'll find a donut on the table and your lunch is in the fridge. See you tonight.

Love – Your Mom and the Monster.

Their note was handwritten.

When I got home that night, my parents made out like nothing had happened. Sometimes they are sneakier than I am. I told them the whole story (and they laughed a lot), and then told them to forget about the VR kit. They really fooled me, when they said yes to my new request! That weekend we built a sukkah. The monster and I even froze sleeping out in it together.

By the way, the VR kit works great. Frankenstein even uses it. It turns out that they had already bought it for me two weeks before this whole thing happened. It was even in the usual place, Frankenstein's dresser drawer. I just had to wait until my birthday.

I'm sorry but that's the end of the story and I've got to go. The Monster will kill me if he catches me with the lights on.

The End, by Marc with a "C" Zeiger.

P.S. I got ninety-seven out of a hundred words right on the spelling test. So much for studying.